THE TSAR'S PROMISE

A Russian Tale retold by
ROBERT D. SAN SOUCI

illustrated by LAUREN MILLS

Philomel Books   New York

A note about the text: The Tsar's Promise was inspired by "King Kojata" in
Andrew Lang's classic *The Green Fairy Book*, first published in London in 1893.
The author has also drawn on other versions of the tale, including Slavic,
Russian, and English, to create this book.

Philomel Books, a division of The Putnam & Grosset Group,
200 Madison Avenue, New York, NY 10016. Published simultaneously in Canada.
Printed in Hong Kong by South China Printing Co. (1988) Ltd.
The text is set in Garamond #3.

Library of Congress Cataloging-in-Publication Data
San Souci, Robert D.   The Tsar's promise
retold by Robert San Souci; illustrated by Lauren Mills. p.   cm.
Summary: The Tsar's son outwits a powerful demon
with the aid of a beautiful princess.
ISBN 0-399-21581-6
[1. Fairy tales. 2. Folklore—Soviet Union.] I. Mills, Lauren
A., ill. II. Title.   PZ8.S248Ts   1992
398.2'1'0947—dc19   [E]   88-22411 CIP AC

1   3   5   7   9   10   8   6   4   2
First Impression

To my good friend, Nancy Bronstein
—R.S.S.

For my father, who never wore a beard.
—L.M.

In Russia there was once a tsar named Kojata, whose flaxen beard was his pride and joy. He let it grow so long that it reached below his knees. Though he and his wife, the tsaritsa, loved each other dearly, the fact that heaven had sent them no child made them sad.

One day the tsar told his wife, "I must journey throughout my kingdom to see how things fare."

After eight months of traveling, he found himself at the edge of a vast forest. The fiery sun gave the tsar a tormenting thirst, so he rode into the woods in search of water. Near sunset he came upon a clear lake. He plunged his face, beard and all, into the cool water, drinking deeply.

When he tried to stand up, however, something held his beard below the water's surface.

"What deviltry is this?" cried the tsar. "Let me go!" Terrified, he saw a horrible face grinning at him from the depths. It had two great green eyes, glowing like emeralds, a nose like a hawk's bill, and a mouth that reached from ear to ear. Powerful claws gripped the ruler's beard.

A voice gurgled from the lake, "Tsar Kojata, I will let you go only if you promise to give me what you will find waiting for you when you return home."

Eager to be free, and thinking there was nothing in his palace worth risking his life for, the tsar answered quickly, "Yes, yes! I promise you shall have it, whatever it is."

The voice replied, "So be it."

The claws relaxed, and the face sank deep into the water and disappeared. Tsar Kojata stood up, mounted his horse, and decided to return home at once.

There he was met by the tsaritsa, who placed in his arms the son born to him during his long absence. The ruler kissed the child and placed a gold cross around the infant's neck, forgetting, in his joy, his promise to the demon.

The tsarevitch, whose name was Ivan, grew into a handsome youth, the pride of his parents.

One day, while he was hunting in a forest far from home, he came upon a lake as clear as crystal. Thirty ducks, with brilliant white feathers, swam on the lake's smooth surface. The young man saw as many white garments set out in a row along the shore. Dismounting, he took one of these and hid behind a nearby bush.

As he watched, the ducks swam to the shore. Twenty-nine of them touched their soft white garments, instantly turned into beautiful maidens, and sank into the earth. Only the thirtieth sat upon the shore and called in a sad human voice, "I was told you would come. If you would kindly return my robe to me, I will tell you a strange story and ask you a great favor."

Ivan set the little garment on the bank beside the duck. As soon as she stepped upon it, the duck became a beautiful girl in a white robe. She was so fair and smiled so sweetly that the young man was speechless.

"My name is Maria," she said. "My sisters and I were stolen from our father, the king of a distant country, by the demon who lives beneath this lake. The wicked creature has a claim upon you through your father. He has ordered me to bring you to him. But I have secretly watched you in his dark mirror, and I have fallen in love with you. Though his power compels me to bring you to him now, together we will find a way to escape. Will you come with me?"

The tsarevitch, in love with the maiden from first sight, agreed.

The girl took his hand, stamped her foot, and the ground opened around them. Together they sank into a huge cavern under the earth.

At the center of the vast open space was a palace, carved from a single ruby. Maria led Ivan through ivory gates to an immense room, where a demon sat upon a golden throne. With a wave of his claw, he ordered Maria to leave.

"Welcome to my kingdom," laughed the demon. "A long time ago, your father promised you to me." The demon went on to explain about Tsar Kojata's hasty promise.

"If my father made such a vow, I shall honor it," said the tsarevitch.

"Excellent! But," the monster went on, "for causing me to wait so long, you must perform three small tasks. Complete them successfully, and you shall win your freedom. Fail, and you forfeit your head."

Ivan asked, "What is the first task?"

"You must build me a palace in one night," said the demon. "The roof must be pure gold; the walls, marble; and the windows, crystal. You must set it in a garden filled with flowers and trees, fishponds and fountains. Do this, and you are one step nearer to your freedom. But if you do not, I will have your head."

The demon had his troll servants escort Ivan to a room with two high-arched windows. A huge mirror in a gold frame stood between them. Though a table was laden with savory food and a goblet of green wine, the tsarevitch could not eat. He sat touching the gold cross at his throat, brooding over the doom his father had unwittingly brought upon him.

Toward evening a bee flew into the room where, as Ivan watched, it turned into the lovely Maria.

"Good evening, Tsarevitch Ivan," she said. "What are you ponder-
ing that makes you so sad?"

"How can I help being sad," he replied, "when I am going to lose my
head in the morning?"

"Have you forgotten that I promised to help you? Do not grieve. I
have learned some of the demon's magic myself. Go to bed, and when
you wake up tomorrow, the palace will be finished. All you must do is
walk around it, tapping on the walls as if you built it yourself."

As the jewels that lit the cavern brightened the morning to begin the underworld's day, Ivan stepped out of his room and found a magnificent palace, exactly as Maria had promised. When the demon arrived, he found Ivan inspecting the marble walls, as if he had just finished the work.

"You certainly have an eye for beauty," said the amazed demon, "so my second challenge will test just how keen your eye is. Tomorrow, I will have thirty beautiful princesses who are sisters stand before you in a row. You must walk past them three times, and then pick out the Princess Maria."

This time Ivan returned to his room in fine spirits and ate all the food set out for him. "It will be the easiest thing in the world to recognize my beautiful Maria," he said aloud.

"Ah, me! That may not be as easy as you imagine," said the little bee, hovering beside his ear. "We are thirty sisters so exactly alike that our own father could hardly tell us apart."

"Then what am I to do?" cried the tsarevitch.

"You will recognize me by a tiny fly I shall have on my left cheek." So saying, she flew away.

The following morning, the magician had Ivan brought to his throne room. There the thirty princesses stood silently in a row, all dressed exactly alike in rich brocade gowns woven with tiny birds and bright flowers.

"Now," said the demon, "look carefully at these beauties three times, and tell me which is the Princess Maria."

Ivan walked past, studying each young woman. But they were all so alike, they seemed one face reflected in thirty mirrors. And the promised fly was nowhere to be seen.

The second time he viewed them, he still saw no insect. Ivan grew worried, as the demon chuckled behind him.

But the third time, he saw a little fly brushing one fair cheek. Immediately, the young man seized the girl's hand and shouted, "This is the Princess Maria!"

"That is right," said the monster angrily. "Now you must do one more thing to gain your freedom." He held up a tiny gold casket. "Tomorrow morning, you must tell me what marvelous marvel is inside here, or lose your life."

Ivan returned to his room. When Maria came to him in the fading jewel-light of evening, he said, "Surely you can find out what wondrous wonder is in the gold casket."

"Alas!" she shook her head sadly. "That secret is protected with a magic spell none can break."

"Then I shall lose my head," he said miserably.

"No, dear Ivan," said Maria. "I love you so much that I shall either save your life or die with you. We must escape now. There is a church

that marks the limit of the demon's power. If we can reach it, we will be safe. Come with me."

Then she breathed on the mirror, capturing his reflection in the glass. Locking the door behind them, they hurried to the spot where they had descended into the lower world. There, the princess stamped her foot, and they returned to the shore of the lake.

Ivan's charger was grazing near the water. The two quickly mounted and sped toward the distant church that was their only hope of escape.

In the meantime, the demon sent his wretched servants to fetch the tsarevitch. They found Ivan's door locked. When they knocked, Ivan's reflection called out from the mirror, "I will be there in a little while." So they returned to the throne room.

After a long wait, the demon again sent his servants to bring the young man before him. A second time, the reflection answered sharply, "I will be there soon enough. Tell your master to bide his time."

At this, the demon lost all patience and commanded the door be broken down. When the servants burst into the room, the reflection laughed at them, then vanished.

Howling with rage, the demon gave his minions horrible beasts to ride, and sent them to the surface to catch Ivan and Maria.

Farther along the road, the tsarevitch said, "I hear the sounds of pursuit close behind us!"

"I will use what magic I have, and we must pray it will be enough to save us," cried Maria. Then she cast a spell that changed her into a river, Ivan into a wooden bridge, and the charger into a blackbird. Beyond the bridge, the road branched three ways.

When the magician's servants came to the bridge, they milled around in confusion because the charger's hoofprints had stopped suddenly, and they did not know which of the three roads to follow. They returned to their master, trembling, and told him what had happened.

"Oh, you fools!" screamed the monster. "They were the river and the bridge. Bring them back at once, or I will punish you terribly!"

The pursuit began again.

Ahead, Ivan and Maria were racing across a meadow. "I hear hoofbeats only a little way behind us," shouted Ivan.

Once more Maria wove a spell, turning herself, Ivan, and his charger into a thick forest.

Their pursuers entered the woods but searched for them in vain. In despair, they returned once more with empty hands to the demon.

"I shall go after the wretches myself!" he bellowed.

Then he mounted a chimera with a lion's head, the body of a goat, and a dragon's tail. With his servants, he rose to the surface and took up the chase.

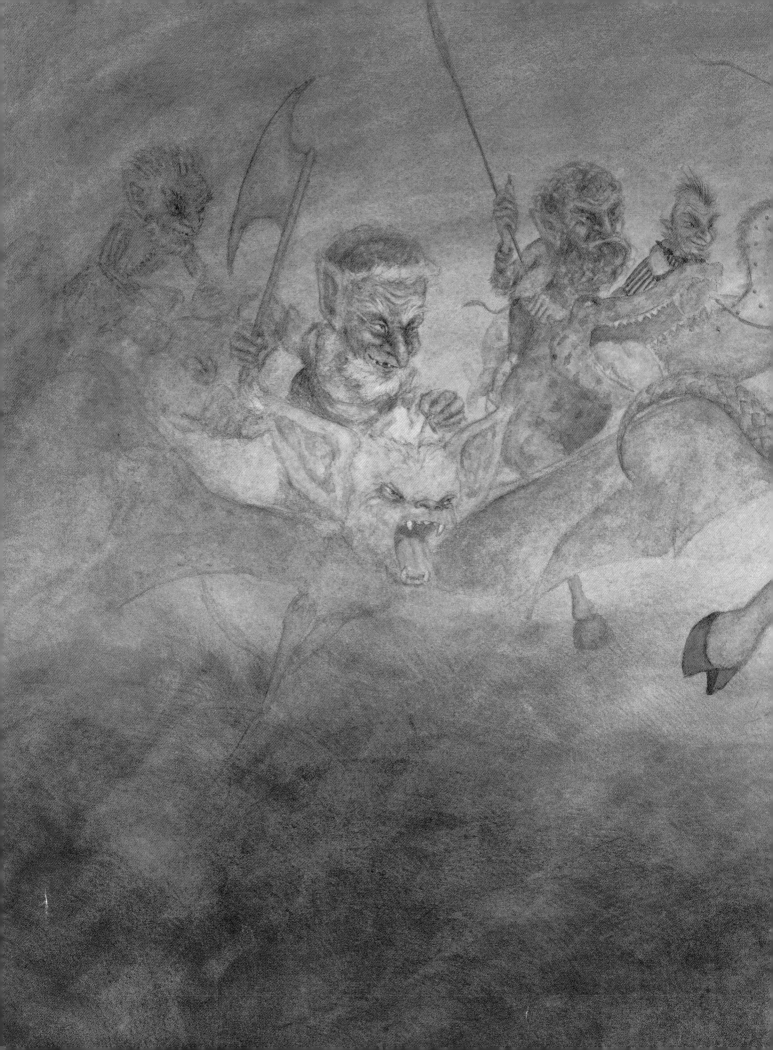

Not far ahead, Ivan warned, "I hear the sounds of pursuit!"

"I recognize the roar of the demon's mount," said Maria. "Now we have only a single chance remaining. Give me the gold cross from around your neck."

Clasping the cross in her hand, Maria changed herself into a little church, the horse into a steeple, and Ivan into a monk. Moments later, the demon and his troop appeared.

Since the church looked like the one that marked the limit of his power, the demon halted at its steps. Because the cross's blessing was mixed with Maria's magic, he could not see through the trick.

"Did a young man and woman on horseback come this way?" he demanded of the monk, who was really Ivan in disguise.

"Yes," said Ivan. "They stopped just long enough to ask me to say a prayer for you."

At this, the demon turned himself and his followers into a swarm of hornets that flew angrily back the way they had come.

But Ivan and Maria continued on until they reached the real church and safety. Soon after this, they returned to the country of Tsar Kojata. There, Ivan and Maria were married, and they lived happily and prospered the rest of their lives.